POISON!

First published in 2014 by Wayland

Wayland
338 Euston Road
London NW1 3BH

Wayland Australia
Level 17/207 Kent Street
Sydney, NSW 2000

Consultant: Dee Reid
Editor: Nicola Edwards
Designer: Alyssa Peacock

A CIP catalogue record for this book is available from the British Library.

Bullies and the beast. – (Freestylers data beast; 4)
823.9'2-dc23

ISBN: 978 0 7502 8230 7
E-book ISBN: 978 0 7502 8815 6

Printed in China

Wayland is a division of Hachette Children's Books,
an Hachette UK Company
www.hachette.co.uk

POISON!

Andrew Fusek Peters
and Alex McArdell

WAYLAND
www.waylandbooks.co.uk

Titles in the series

Bats!

978 0 7502 8231 4

Bullies and the Beast

978 0 7502 8229 1

Monster Savings

978 0 7502 8232 1

Poison!

978 0 7502 8230 7

CHAPTER 1

"What is that horrible smell?" asked Roz.

We were in my kitchen.

"It could be coming from the chemical factory up the road," I said. "That place smells rank!"

Data Beast was mending the oven. He was great at DIY! Roz had created Data Beast on her computer. At first he was scary, but now he was a sort-of pet. A pet monster made of numbers.

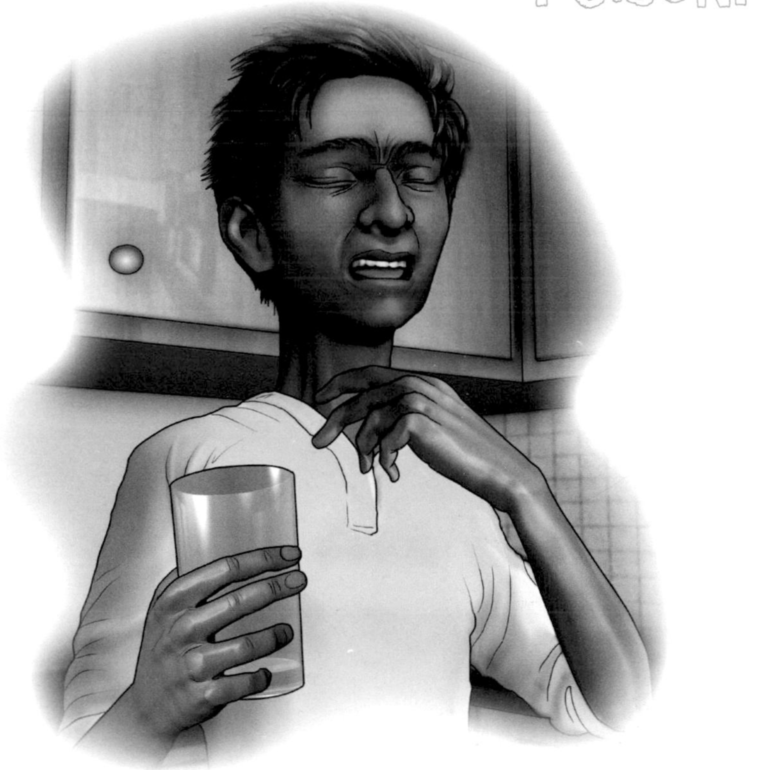

I poured some water from the tap and gulped it down. I began to cough.

"Help!" I said.

"Get a grip!" Roz laughed.

"No joke, " I gasped. "Can't... breathe!" My throat was burning.

I started falling slowly towards the floor. Data Beast was staring at me with his black eyes. Then he was flying through the air towards my head. I felt a tickle in my ear. After that, nothing.

"Kiran! Wake up!" shouted Roz.

"Ow! Don't slap me!" I said. The slap hurt me but at least it meant I was still alive.

"What happened?" I asked.

"You passed out!" said Roz.

"I know," I said, "but what did Data Beast do? He was heading straight for me!"

"It was amazing," said Roz. "He dived into your ear!"

I shivered all over and sat up.

"Why would he do that?" I asked.

Data Beast shook his head.

"You drink bad stuff," he said.

"But water is good for you!" I argued.

"This water not good," said Data Beast. "Had to go in."

"What do you mean?" I asked. "This is freaking me out!"

"Had to go inside you. Do … DIY repair," said Data Beast. "

"Wow," I said to Data Beast. "I thought I was dying. You saved me."

"The chemical factory must be poisoning the water," said Roz grimly.

"Yes," I said. "Look out of the window."

Two huge cooling towers hung over the skyline. Thick streams of smoke poured out.

"We must tell the police," I said. "We need to show them the evidence." I ran to the sink and turned on the tap. But now the water smelled fine.

"Evidence... gone," said Data Beast.

CHAPTER 2

The next day, I kept feeling my neck and throat. They felt fine thanks to Data Beast.

I boiled the kettle five times before I made a cup of tea. I also told my mum that the water was dodgy. She said I was making stuff up as usual.

When I got home from school, I looked through the local paper.

There was a picture of a man in a smart suit. He was the new boss at the chemical factory. He was saying how he was going to save the company lots of money.

On another page of the paper I saw a headline: *Mystery death of hundreds of fish.* There was a picture of the river that ran behind the fields on the edge of town. I'd been there a few times, but fishing wasn't my thing.

I texted Roz to come over quickly.

When she arrived. I showed her the picture of the dead fish.

"So what?" she said.

"I think the chemical factory is putting poison in the river and that is what is killing all the fish." I said.

"Of course," I said, "they say it's not them. They say they can prove the poison comes from elsewhere."

"I bet they are lying," said Roz.

"Well, they nearly killed me yesterday," I said. "It's payback time."

"By the way, where's Data Beast?" I asked Roz.

"He is having a snooze inside my tablet," said Roz. "I downloaded hundreds of pages of numbers from the internet. He's made himself a nest with them."

“Here he is, look!” Roz said. Roz showed me a folder on her screen. She tapped it twice and suddenly streams of numbers and signs began flowing past.

There was Data Beast, curled up inside a nest of numbers.

"He is so sweet, isn't he?" smiled Roz.

"I would never call Data Beast sweet!" I said. "Anyway, wake him up. We have got work to do!"

CHAPTER 3

We hid behind the bins beside the fence outside the chemical factory.

"We must be mad," I whispered to Roz. "This is an electric fence. There are guards everywhere. And we are just two teenagers!"

"Are you wimping out on me?" Roz whispered back.

"Anyway, we don't need to go inside the factory. We can just stay here, behind the fence," said Roz.

"How?" I asked her.

Roz was tapping away on her tablet.

"Listen and learn from an expert hacker!" she said.

Suddenly the image of Data Beast was on the screen. He gave me the thumbs up.

"Data Beast can hitch a lift on any device," said Roz. "All we need is someone going on site."

At that moment, a woman in a suit walked past. She was talking into a mobile phone.

I looked back at Roz's tablet. Data Beast had gone.

Suddenly the screen showed the gate of the factory getting closer. We had a real live feed!

It didn't take long for Data Beast to hop through the wi-fi and skip straight into the labs deep inside the factory.

We watched the screen. Behind a set of swing doors, we could see a huge tank of water. Data Beast took a step towards it. The tank was full of fish, all floating round slowly.

"Fish not well!" we heard Data Beast say.

"We need to smuggle them out as proof," I said.

Roz turned back to the screen.

"Get the data!" she whispered.

Data Beast set to work. It looked like lightning was flickering through all the servers and computers.

It didn't take long.

"I have... all the lies! Now must go!" said Data Beast. A woman in a white coat pushed open the swing doors. Data Beast vanished. Seconds later, he was crouching beside us.

"Everything... in my memory," he said.

CHAPTER 4

As Data Beast spoke, an alarm began to blare and spotlights went on. We were in big trouble.

"Run!" shouted Roz.

We ran. I wondered how the chemical company knew what we had done.

"Clever computer!" said Data Beast. It was as if he could read my mind.

"I trip over. Inside mainframe. Mistake. Computer saw me."

We sprinted down an alley. I heard a car screech behind us.

"Oh no!" I said. "It's a dead end! What do we do now?"

The car came straight at us. We put our hands up. At the last second, the car skidded to a stop. Its headlights shone in our eyes.

"Stupid kids," a man's voice said. "Messing with our machines. Think they need a lesson. A violent one."

"This is not looking good!" I hissed. "Where is Data Beast when we need him?"

"Hey!" said one of the men. "What's happening?"

The headlights smashed. Then the car began to rock from side to side.

"Leave it out!" screamed another man.

The car rocked faster and faster. Suddenly it was upside down.

Data Beast crouched on the ground and stared at the men.

"Bad ones trapped!" he roared.

"Yes, they are!" we laughed.

CHAPTER 5

The police didn't believe us at first. But we had all the data, downloaded from Data Beast. The factory was shut down while the poisonous leak was fixed.

"I reckon those chemicals are making the workers crazy," said the police officer. "We picked up one worker for dangerous driving. He had turned his car over but he kept saying a monster had done it!"

Roz and I tried not to look at each other.

That night, Data Beast got us into the factory. The place was strange. There was nobody around. In the lab, the fish were still there, but they were almost dead.

"Poison," said Data Beast. "I must do... best..."

I saw Data Beast dissolve like sugar, into a river of code. He flowed into the pool of fish. The water sparked like fireflies. It only took a second before the fish perked up and began swimming around again.

Data Beast streamed out again. At first, he was just a pool of black muck on the floor. Then he slowly took shape.

"Took out poison," he gasped. "Ate... it. Hurts. Maybe... die."

I felt tears in my eyes. So uncool.

"We have to heal him," I told Roz.

"Got it! He loves numbers. We need to surround him with numbers."

"What do you mean?" she asked.

"Do a search," I said.

Roz whipped out her tablet and tapped away.

"I think I've found something," she said.

Music came from the tablet. It sounded like children singing the 2x table.

The effect on Data Beast was amazing.

He sat up straight. Then he began to sway from side to side in time to the music.

"Very... calm," murmured Data Beast. "Like... it."

I rubbed my eyes. I didn't want anyone to see my tears.

"Good to have you back," was all I could say.

Returning the fish to the river was easy. Roz found a local wildlife rescue centre who brought a truck with a huge tank. It was brilliant to see the fish sliding into the safe, clean water of the river.

As the truck drove off, we stood by the water's edge. The moon shone down.

"Good work!" I told Data Beast.

"And you...," he said to me. "When I hurt... you helped me!"

" Do you hear that?" I asked Roz. "At least Data Beast appreciates me!"

FOR TEACHERS

Freestylers is a series of carefully levelled stories, especially geared for struggling readers of both sexes. With very low reading age and high interest age, these books are humorous, fun, up-to-the-minute and edgy. Core characters provide familiarity in all of the stories, build confidence and ease pupils from one story through to the next, accelerating reading progress.

Freestylers can be used for both guided and independent reading. To make the most of the books you can:

• Focus on making each reading session successful. Talk about the text before the pupil starts reading. Introduce the characters, the storyline and any unfamiliar vocabulary.

• Encourage the pupil to talk about the book during reading and after reading. How would they have felt if they were Kiran? Or Roz? How would they have reacted to the problem of pollution in their local area?

• Talk about which parts of the story they like best and why.

For guidance, this story has been approximately measured to:

National Curriculum Level: 2A
Reading Age: 8.6
Book Band: White

ATOS: 3.0
Lexile ® Measure [confirmed]: 380L